# WITHDRAWN
# Shu-Li
## and
# Tamara

# Shu-Li

By
Paul Yee

and Tamara

Illustrated by
Shaoli Wang

Vancouver  London

Published in 2007 in Canada and Great Britain by
Tradewind Books • www.tradewindbooks.com

Distribution and representation in Canada by
Publishers Group Canada • www.pgcbooks.ca

Distribution and representation in the UK by
Turnaround • www.turnaround-uk.com

Text copyright © 2007 by Paul Yee
Illustrations copyright © 2007 by Shaoli Wang
Book & cover design by Jacqueline Wang

Printed in Canada on 100% ancient forest friendly paper.
2 4 6 8 10 9 7 5 3 1

Cataloguing-in-Publication Data for this book
is available from The British Library.

Library and Archives Canada Cataloguing in Publication

Yee, Paul
    Shu-Li and Tamara / by Paul Yee ; illustrated by Shaoli Wang.

ISBN 978-1-896580-93-7

    I. Wang, Shaoli, 1961-  II. Title.

PS8597.E3S58 2007          jC813'.54          C2007-903778-X

*For Shaila, who will write books — PY*

*To Tao Hong, for our common dream — SW*

*The publisher acknowledges the support of the Canada Council for the Arts.*

 **Canada Council** **Conseil des Arts**
**for the Arts** **du Canada**

*The publisher also wishes to thank the Government of British Columbia for the financial support it has extended through the book publishing tax credit program and the British Columbia Arts Council.*

 BRITISH COLUMBIA
ARTS COUNCIL
Supported by the Province of British Columbia

*The publisher also acknowledges the financial support of the Government of Canada through the Book Publishing Industry Development Program (BPIDP) and the Association for the Export of Canadian Books (AECB) for our publishing activities.*

# Chapter One

Every Saturday, Shu-Li worked at her parents' shop, the Yum Yum Chinese Deli. They told her to keep the serving counter clean and to take the empty dishes off the tables.

Shu-Li stopped and looked out the front window when the ice-cream boy pedalled by on his cart ringing his bell. Children were playing tag on Commercial Drive, laughing and shouting under the blue sky. Shoppers hurried by with shopping bags and cake boxes. Tyrone, a boy from Shu-Li's class at school, swung by on his skateboard.

Shu-Li sighed and wished she could stop work and race outside. She loved living near the Drive. When she arrived at her new school, her teacher, Mr. Ortega, said, "You're lucky to be living there! It's full of neat stores and nice parks. It's a fun neighbourhood."

Six months ago, Shu-Li's family moved out of her uncle's house in Richmond. She became so busy with schoolwork, piano and the deli that she didn't have time to explore her new neighbourhood.

Before her family came to Canada from China, Shu-Li's father, Ba, had worked as a chef. Now he ran the deli, cooking dishes such as stir-fried greens, spicy chicken and beef and tofu. The food smelled so good that customers found it hard to choose from the steaming trays. They also fussed over which soup, dessert or sweet bubble tea they might buy.

Sometimes people asked Ba to prepare large

pans of food for parties and celebrations. Shu-Li
was happy when that happened, because then
there wasn't any clean-up work for her to do.

All of a sudden three girls trooped in from
the park, chattering in loud voices.

"Shu-Li!" exclaimed Hannah. "I didn't
know you worked here." Hannah was with her
friends Shona and Jenna.

Shu-Li's throat went dry. She was too scared
to speak.

The girls were in her grade-four class and wore the trendiest clothing. If you saw one of them, the other two were close by. They did everything together: homework, lunch and class projects. They walked each other to school and called themselves the *Nah-Nah Girls*. Rushing to the counter, they stared at the cookies.

"Welcome you to Yum Yum Deli," called out Ma.

The girls burst out laughing.

Shu-Li's face reddened. How many times had she told Ma not to use the word *you* in that sentence? But her mother still spoke as if she were translating the ideas directly from Chinese.

"What's that?" Shona pointed.

"Almond," said Ma.

"And that one?"

"Coconut." Ma smiled and pointed to Shona's shirt. "I like green colour."

The girls smirked.

"I like green colour too," Shona repeated.

The girls giggled loudly.

Shu-Li avoided eye contact with the girls and furiously scrubbed the counter.

*Good thing they don't want to be my friends,* she thought. *I could never make friends with people who laugh at my mother.*

After the deli emptied, Shu-Li hurried into

the kitchen. Ba and Ma sat at the table eating Singapore noodles from the lunch menu. Ba scooped some noodles into a dish for her.

*Yummy!* Shu-Li thought. Singapore noodles were her favourite. Often they were the first thing to be sold out.

"Can I go to the park?" Shu-Li asked in Chinese.

"Who with?" demanded Ba.

"Alone."

"You can't go by yourself," said Ba.

"But you said I could go after I finished cleaning up."

"Listen to your father, Shu-Li," said Ma.

# Chapter Two

On Monday morning Mr. Ortega asked, "Grade fours, how many more weeks of school are left?"

"Two!" shouted the class.

"Are we ready for this year's school fair?"

"Yes!" yelled everyone.

"After the fair we'll spend a week doing field trips."

"Hooray!"

Shu-Li sat quietly at the back. She had enrolled halfway through the term, and it hadn't been easy for her to make friends. The popular girls sat among themselves, passed notes to each other and told jokes back and forth. The *Nah-Nah Girls* thought they were smarter than anyone else in the class. Joey Zhao sat with his pal Tyrone. Both of them were troublemakers. Mr. Ortega often sent them to see the principal, Ms Kumar.

Joey's parents owned a house in the neighbourhood and rented the upstairs to Shu-Li's family. His family lived on the ground floor.

- SCHOOL FAIR IN TWO WEEKS

- FIELD TRIPS

The parents of both children wanted them to become friends, but that hadn't happened.

"So, boys and girls, where shall we go?" Mr. Ortega asked.

When all the children started shouting at once, Mr. Ortega held up his hands and silenced the class. "Everyone can suggest a place, and all ideas will be taken seriously. So speak up, but one at a time, please."

Joey waved his hand furiously. "The ice-cream factory!" he called out.

The students shouted, "Me too! Free samples!"

"Can we go to Splashdown Water Park?" someone asked.

"Can we go?" pleaded the others. "Please?"

Mr. Ortega frowned. "It's a bit far away, but we'll put it on the list."

"How about IMAX at Science World?"

"How about Play Palace?"

"How about Grouse Mountain?"

"Can we go to the Buddhist temple?" asked Tamara. She had just moved to the neighbourhood.

"No way!" Hannah made a face.

"That's no fun!" Shona exclaimed.

"That's not for kids!" Jenna shouted.

"It's a great idea," Mr. Ortega said. "I'll look into it."

Shu-Li wanted to make a suggestion, but her hands were shaking. They always trembled when she had to speak out.

Mr. Ortega had told her not to be afraid to speak her mind. "Don't worry about being wrong," he had said cheerfully. "That's how we learn."

Ms Kumar once said to her, "In Canada, we want children to speak up in class. You don't need to have the right answer here. We expect everyone to join in the discussions."

*Why am I so scared?* Shu-Li thought. *Ma isn't afraid to talk to her customers at the deli, even though her English is terrible.*

"How about the Yoga Centre?" Shu-Li finally blurted out.

There was a moment of silence, followed by Joey's loud voice. "That's so dumb. Yoga's for girls."

"No it's not," Shu-Li said, her voice rising. "Yoga's for everyone!"

*I'm not dumb*, she thought, glaring at Joey. *He's the one who's dumb. How could Ma and Ba think Joey and I would ever become friends?*

"I'm not going!" Tyrone shouted out.

"I never eat yogurt," added someone else.

Everyone laughed loudly.

# Chapter Three

"Shu-Li, did you see me race Tyrone?" shouted Joey, rushing into the deli. "He didn't have a chance!"

Shu-Li didn't bother to answer him. He always talked on and on about himself and how well he did at sports. Joey came to the deli every day after school and waited around until his parents picked him up after work. That was the only time he was friendly with Shu-Li.

"Oh, hello, Auntie," Joey said to Shu-Li's mother. He was always polite to *her* because she gave him free snacks.

"Say hello to Constable Rooney," Ma said.

Jane Rooney from the Community Policing

Centre was chatting with a woman Shu-Li had never seen before. The officer looked imposing in her uniform and cap. Her badge was silvery and shiny. Her leather belt gleamed.

"Hello, Constable Rooney," Joey said.

"Hi, Joey. What are you kids doing for the school fair?"

"My project is called *Kids Helping Kids*," Shu-Li said. "We're raising money to help a village in Africa buy goats."

"That's wonderful. I'll be looking for your table. What about you, Joey?"

"I'm doing breakdancing."

"Great, I'll come and see you perform. Thanks for the bubble tea, Mrs. Wu. Welcome to the Drive, Mrs. Richards."

Constable Rooney waved goodbye and left.

"Say hello to Mrs. Richards," Ma said to Shu-Li. "She just moved to here with her daughter."

"Not *to* here, Ma," Shu-Li said. "Just *here*."

The door to the bathroom opened and a girl came out.

"Hi, Tamara," Shu-Li said.

"You two know each other?" Mrs. Richards asked.

"We're working on the same project for the school fair," said Tamara. "Hi, Shu-Li!"

The two girls were the same height, but Tamara was thinner. Freckles dotted her face. Her T-shirt was too small, and her shorts were too large.

"Here's your order," Ma said, pushing forward a bag. "Fourteen dollars, please."

Mrs. Richards opened her purse. "Uh-oh," she said. "I only have ten dollars. I'd better leave out the spring rolls."

Tamara blushed and looked away. Shu-Li knew how awful it felt when your own mother embarrassed you in front of other children.

"Don't worry," said Ma.

"I'll go to the bank and be right back."

"Don't worry. You can pay next time."

"Why, thank you. You're very kind. That's the nicest thing I've heard in a long time. You were going to tell me what's in your recipe for spicy chicken."

Joey grabbed Shu-Li's arm and pulled her outside. "That Tamara is trouble," he said after the door closed behind them. "Hannah said that the day after she joined our class ten dollars went missing from her jacket pocket. And Tamara sits right next to her!"

"Really?" Shu-Li was surprised.

"She steals!"

"What proof do you have?"

"Look, you saw. Her mother can't even afford to pay for food. Of course Tamara steals."

Shu-Li didn't want to listen to Joey. She went inside just in time to hear Mrs. Richards say, "I'm going to the bank to get some money, Tamara. Do you want to come with me or stay here with your friend?"

"I'd like to stay," Tamara said.

Shu-Li beamed at those words.

"Take Tamara into the kitchen," Ma said with a smile.

Shu-Li was horrified. "I can't take her back there!" she exclaimed.

But customers were coming in, so Ma shooed the girls into the kitchen.

# Chapter Four

Ba was hard at work, stirring a wok full of crackling, sizzling fish with black bean sauce. The smell of hot oil and black beans filled the air. When the girls stumbled in, he spun around, accidentally knocking a bowl off the counter. It smashed to pieces, and the girls jumped at the sound. A white sauce spread long fingers across the floor.

"Who's this?" he demanded in Chinese.

"My friend," said Shu-Li.

"She can't be in here! Take her out!"

"But Ma told us to come in…"

"Go! Now!"

The girls darted out through the front of the deli and into the street before Ma could stop them.

*How could Ba have been so rude?* Shu-Li fretted. *Now Tamara won't want to be my friend.*

"I made him break a dish!" Tamara cried out, as if she were about to burst into tears. "Your father won't want me back here again."

"It's his busy time right now. If we go back later, it'll be fine. Don't worry."

"Was he swearing at me?"

"Don't worry."

"Stop saying *don't worry*! It's making me crazy."

The two girls sat on the sidewalk bench facing the park and watched the trolley rumble by. The power cable made a rubbery rolling sound.

Then both girls spoke at the same time.

"My mom does yoga but not at the Yoga Centre," Tamara said.

"My mother's friend goes to the Buddhist temple," Shu-Li said.

They stopped and grinned at one another.

"Do you think we'll get to visit the places we suggested?" Tamara asked.

"Maybe, but I sure don't want the boys to go. As soon as we get there, they'll want to leave."

"Boys!"

"Ugh!"

They both rolled their eyes toward the sky.

"I love Chinese food. Does your dad make spring rolls? That's my favourite."

"My father says fried foods aren't healthy." Shu-Li frowned.

"What about won-ton soup? Why does it have that name? Does it weigh a ton?"

Shu-Li had heard Ma explain this to her customers. "In Chinese, won-ton means swallowing clouds. It's because the dumpling looks like a cloud."

"Yes, white and round."

"I like hot-and-sour soup more."

"I don't like spicy food."

"It's not spicy. It just tastes good."

The girls fell silent again.

"Have you been to the ice-cream factory?" Shu-Li asked. "It's not far from here."

Tamara shook her head. "Not yet."

"People say it has over two hundred flavours. Do you think it's true?"

"Two hundred?"

"That's what I hear."

"Then that Joey had a good idea."

"Just one."

They burst out laughing.

# Chapter Five

Every day after school that week Tamara went with Shu-Li to the deli and helped out. Their first job was to pluck parsley leaves from the stalks.

"Your fingers are thin, Tamara. That is good," Ba said. "My fingers are thick, so I leave on too much stalk. Then my daughter has to do them again."

"Can I try making won-ton too?" Tamara asked.

"Sure! It's easy," Ba said. "Put meat onto the wrapper, flip the stick over twice and pull it out. Bend the wrapper ends back and then fasten

them together with a dab of water."

Soon Tamara rolled perfect dumplings.

The girls shelled and skinned peanuts from big bulky bags. When Ba wasn't looking, Shu-Li threw peanuts in the air, and Tamara tried to catch them in her mouth. But most of them landed on the floor.

When they finished their chores, the girls walked up the Drive together. They loved the smell of handmade chocolates, Ethiopian coffee and Italian pastries. The street was always crowded with people shopping for Latin American crafts, old and new books, Cuban food and Italian sausages.

One day, they visited the shoe store and left behind twenty boxes for the clerk to put away. Another day, they tried on sunglasses at the eyeglass store. The owner had to follow them

around, wiping each pair of glasses after their fingers left smudges on the lenses. Usually they looked through the CDs at the music store. But one day they accidentally knocked over the window display.

Tamara had no money to buy anything that cost a lot, but she always had pocket money to treat Shu-Li to ice cream or pizza.

"Joey's father says that Tamara steals money,"
said Ba one evening, coming into Shu-Li's room.

"There's no proof."

"Are you sure?"

"She's my friend."

"You be careful," he
warned.

The next night
Tamara's mom
invited Shu-Li
over for dinner,
but Ba didn't
want her to go.

"Of course
she will go," Ma
said. "Tamara is
Shu-Li's best
friend!"

Shu-Li silently thanked her mother and promised herself never to get mad at Ma again for making mistakes when she spoke English.

Shu-Li was surprised at how small Tamara's apartment was. There was only one bedroom. The kitchen and the living room were tiny, and there wasn't much space for furniture. She noticed that there were no books or newspapers lying around.

"Where do you sleep?" Shu-Li asked.

"Right here," Tamara explained, sitting down on the couch. "This is my bed."

She opened a family photo album and showed it to Shu-Li.

"Is this your father?" Shu-Li asked, pointing at a picture in the album.

"No, that's my uncle. My mother took out all the pictures of my father. They haven't spoken to each other since they got divorced."

Tamara's mother served macaroni and cheese along with salad and cranberry juice. Everything was delicious. Shu-Li noticed that even though Tamara's mother did not eat much, there were no leftovers.

*How does Tamara have enough money for ice cream and pizza?* Shu-Li wondered. *Maybe she did steal that money from Hannah.*

That night, when Shu-Li returned home, she asked her mother, "Did Mrs. Richardson ever repay the four dollars she owed?"

"No."

"Doesn't it bother you?"

"No, she buys food from us all the time, and she always pays in full. It's not a problem."

"Why don't you ask her for the money?"

"She's a good customer."

# Chapter Six

Nanwon and Tamara painted a colourful sign
that showed three shaggy goats saying *Help
Raise Money for an African Village to Buy Goats —
Kids Helping Kids*. Shu-Li's class had been getting
ready for the school fair since winter.

Some of her classmates used bamboo and
coloured paper to build lanterns in the shape
of gigantic grasshoppers, fish and eagles for
the parade, while others practised breakdancing
in the hall. They jumped
and twisted to the hit
songs blasting out
from speakers.

Shu-Li and Tamara's group planned to raise money to help a village in Africa buy goats by selling baked goods at the fair. Once a week, they went to the staff room along with Nanwon and Satinder and baked oatmeal-raisin cookies, blueberry muffins and chocolate chip cookies. When the goodies passed the taste test, they were put into the freezer.

The day before the fair, Ba asked, "How about I bake some cookies for your sale?"

"Wonderful!" shouted the girls.

"How about my almond cookies?" he offered.

"They're famous on the Drive," exclaimed Tamara. "I see people eating them all the time."

"Can *we* make the cookies?" asked Shu-Li.

"I can use my mixer," replied Ba. "The dough will be ready in no time."

"We made all the other treats," Shu-Li pointed out.

Ba frowned. "I don't think we have enough time."

"This is about kids helping a village in Africa," pleaded Tamara. "Please, Mr. Wu?"

Ba thought it over. "If we make smaller batches," he said, "then you can each prepare the dough."

The girls grinned at each other.

Ba put a mix of flour and powders into two big bowls. "Use these knives to cut in the shortening," he said. "Like this."

Soon the girls were clicking their knives loudly, making music. After the eggs were added, Ba said, "Use your hands to press the dough together."

"Yuck!" said Tamara. "This is gross!"

"This is fun!" said Shu-Li.

"Your hands will warm the dough and soften it," said Ba. "It's the best way to mix."

Tamara slowly put her hands into the dough and carefully squeezed the mixture. Then she relaxed and smiled.

When the trays of cookies came out of the oven, they smelled delicious. The girls couldn't wait to surprise Nanwon and Satinder with these extra goodies for the sale.

# Chapter Seven

On the morning of the fair, Shu-Li and Tamara made sure all the treats were defrosted and then drew up a list of prices. They wrapped each cookie, muffin and bar in plastic and counted them carefully.

"Where are Nanwon and Satinder?" Shu-Li asked.

"They should be here helping us," Tamara replied.

A huge crowd poured into the school when the festival opened. Costumed musicians on stilts danced high above the ground. An art show of children's paintings and papier-mâché sculpture filled the gymnasium. A TV reporter with special lights and a camera filmed the students practising for the breakdancing

performance. The grade fives displayed their self-published books. The hallway was lined with photographs taken by the grade six class.

"I'm afraid I've got some bad news," Ms Kumar said, rushing up to the girls. "Mr. Ortega was in a car accident last night!"

"No!" Shu-Li groaned.

"He's at the hospital. But he's going to be fine."

"I'm so glad!" Tamara exclaimed.

"But now there's no one to supervise you."

"What about you?" Shu-Li asked.

"I'm working with the breakdancers and the lantern people."

"Why can't we sell the baked goods ourselves?" Tamara asked.

"There's money involved. You need an adult."

"But if we can't sell our goodies," Shu-Li pointed out, "then our village in Africa loses out."

Ms Kumar sighed and thought it over. "Okay, but where are Nanwon and Satinder?"

"Mr. Ortega was supposed to pick them up," Tamara said.

Ms Kumar frowned. Just then Joey passed by. She reached out and grabbed his arm.

"You're going to help these two girls with their table."

"I can't," he protested. "I'm on the breakdance team."

"This is an emergency. Mr. Ortega can't be here, and Nanwon and Satinder aren't here yet. You have to fill in."

"But my team needs me!" Joey stammered. "They won't be able to do their performance."

"You're going to help the girls set up their table and *then* do your breakdancing! As soon as you're done, come back and help with the Africa project," Ms Kumar said in her *this-is-final* voice. "I'll be right back with your cash box, girls."

"This is a lousy idea," Joey growled, slumping down into one of the chairs.

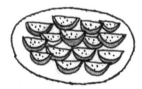

# Chapter
# Eight

$I$t took several trips for Joey and the girls to carry the sign and the trays of food from the staff room to the gym.

"I should be on stage right now!" exclaimed Joey, running off to the auditorium.

Just then, Nanwon

and Satinder came rushing in.

"I'm sorry we're so late," Nanwon said. "Mr. Ortega was supposed to pick us up but never showed up!"

"He was in a car accident," Tamara said.

"But Ms Kumar says he's all right," Shu-Li added quickly.

Nanwon and Satinder sighed in relief.

"Where is everyone?" Satinder asked.

"They're all at the variety show," Shu-Li answered.

"There are so many goodies left," Nanwon said. "Haven't you sold any?"

"We're just getting started," Shu-Li answered. She was pleased when Satinder and Nanwon asked about the almond cookies. Then Shu-Li and Tamara tasted the Indian sweets called *halwa* that Satinder had brought.

"Yummy!" Shu-Li said.

"Yummy!" Tamara repeated.

"I helped make them," said Satinder. "It was easy!"

"What's this?" Jenna made a face as the other two *Nah-Nah Girls* sauntered over behind her.

"Chocolate chip cookies," said Shu-Li. "Want to buy one?"

"It looks like someone sat on them. Yuck!" snickered Jenna.

Hannah and Shona giggled.

"You look like someone sat on *you*," said Tamara.

The *Nah Nah Girls* simply turned around and marched off.

"Thanks, Tamara," said Shu-Li.

"They're so dumb!"

A giant paper dragon with gleaming wings and a spiked tail swooped past, followed by a huge crowd of people.

"The variety show must be over," Tamara said.

Joey came running up. "You should have seen me! I was great. Hey! You guys are going to have a lot of leftovers. You'll end up giving them away."

"Everyone seems to be at all the other tables," Nanwon said.

"Joey, why don't you do your breakdance in front of our table?" Shu-Li suggested.

"No way! There's no music."

"You don't need music. We can all clap, and you can do your moves.

You're so good. People will come to watch!"

"But who's going to do the selling?"

"I will!" Ms Kumar said, walking up to the table and putting on an apron.

The four girls clapped their hands in a tight, quick beat. Joey started to dance. He flattened himself on the floor as if he were about to do push-ups. One leg kicked out, swung in a semi-circle and then twisted underneath him. His entire body flipped over, and then his legs and one arm thrust straight up into the air. Joey looked like he was floating over the floor. He did a handstand, resting on his elbow, and held the pose.

People crowded around to watch and started buying the treats.

Joey's body turned into a blur. One minute he spun like a top with his legs in the air. Then he rolled around on the ground like a log. After that he arched over like a crab. The next minute he flipped himself upright and performed fancy footwork as the crowd joined in with their clapping. Joey's body looked as if it were made out of elastic. When he finally stopped, everyone applauded.

"Help us raise money for children in Africa!" he shouted, pointing to the table of baked goods. Suddenly the table was flooded with customers.

"Are these homemade?" people asked.

"Where in Africa will the money be going?"

"Are there other ways we can help *Kids Helping Kids*?"

"Great job, Joey!" Ms Kumar said, handing him her apron. "I have to go help at another table."

People bought the cookies and Indian sweets non-stop.

"Delicious!" everyone exclaimed.

It didn't take long before the last cookie was sold.

"Yippee!" shouted Satinder.

# Chapter Nine

"Let's count the money," Shu-Li said. "Maybe we have enough for *four* goats!"

They chattered excitedly as they sorted the nickels, dimes and loonies. They set aside the quarters and toonies. They flattened and unfolded the bills. They counted and reached a final total.

"Uh-oh!" Shu-Li frowned. They were short by twenty dollars.

Joey and the girls counted the money again. But the total came up the same.

"What's in your pocket?" Joey demanded,

"Sorry." He looked up at Tamara. "I'm sorry. Really, I am."

"That's okay, Joey," Tamara replied.

Then she put her arm around Shu-Li's shoulders. "Thanks for being on my side, Shu-Li. I never had a friend like you."

"Me neither!"

# Recipes

# Shu-Li's Almond Cookies

¾ cup chopped almonds

½ cup sugar

½ cup butter

1 tablespoon flour

2 tablespoons milk

Preheat oven to 375° F. Have all ingredients at room temperature. Combine all the ingredients in a medium saucepan and cook over low heat until the butter is melted. Drop small teaspoons of the mixture 3 inches apart on a well-greased cookie sheet. Bake until golden brown, approximately 8-9 minutes. Cool slightly and remove from the cookie sheet with a small pancake lifter.

This recipe makes about 2 dozen thin, lacy cookies.

Gertie Tennant's cookie recipe is from
*Chow: From China to Canada: Memories of Food & Family*
by Janice Wong, Whitecap Books, 2005.

# Tamara's Chocolate Chip Cookies

Cream together:

**1 cup margarine**
**¾ cup white sugar**
**¾ cup brown sugar**

Mix in as well:

**1 egg**
**1 tsp. vanilla**

Mix in ½ cup at a time:

**2 ¼ cups white flour**
**½ tsp. baking soda**

Add:

**1 cup chocolate chips**

Using a teaspoon, roll a blob of batter in your hand and place on cookie sheet. Press down ball with two fingers. Bake at 350° F for 13 minutes. Take them out when they don't look done and they will be chewy and delicious.

Recipe from *The Gordon Cookbook,* Gordon School, Vancouver, 1999

glaring at Tamara. "I saw you put something in your pocket."

"I...I didn't take any money," she stammered.

"Shu-Li told me you always have pocket money for ice cream and pizza," Joey pointed out. "Now we know how you get it."

Tamara looked over at Shu-Li for help.

"Check the trays again," Shu-Li said. "Maybe a bill got stuck under one of them."

Joey checked the trays again but found nothing.

"Maybe the money fell on the floor," Satinder said.

They looked under the table. Nothing.

"We should tell Ms Kumar," Joey said.

Just then Constable Rooney walked up.

"Tamara stole money from the

Africa project!" Joey shouted.

"I never stole anything," Tamara said, breaking out in tears.

Shu-Li went over and stood by Tamara. "She never stole anything!" Shu-Li cried out.

"I saw her put money in her pocket. Go ahead and ask her," Joey said.

Constable Rooney turned to Tamara. "Well, what do you have to say to that, young lady?"

Tamara looked down at her feet. She didn't answer. She didn't move. Her hands were bunched in her pockets.

"*I* didn't see her steal anything," Shu-Li said.

"*I* saw her put money in her pocket," Joey said again.

"Are you sure?" Constable Rooney asked.

"Sure, I'm sure. She always has pocket money to spend. Where do you get all that money?" Joey repeated.

Tamara's face reddened as she explained. "My dad gives me money. You can ask him."

"But twenty dollars is still missing!" Joey's lips tightened. He crossed his arms over his chest and glared at Tamara.

"Did you check the pocket of your apron, Joey?" asked Shu-Li.

"Why? I never put any money in my pocket."

"But Ms Kumar was wearing the apron, remember?" Shu-Li said.

"That's right," Satinder said. "Maybe she left it there by accident."

Joey put his hand in the pocket of the apron. Suddenly his face turned red. It was his turn to look at the ground as he pulled out a twenty-dollar bill.

"What do you say *now*, Joey?" Constable Rooney asked.

"Sorry." He looked up at Tamara. "I'm sorry. Really, I am."

"That's okay, Joey," Tamara replied.

Then she put her arm around Shu-Li's shoulders. "Thanks for being on my side, Shu-Li. I never had a friend like you."

"Me neither!"

# Recipes

# Shu-Li's Almond Cookies

¾ cup chopped almonds

½ cup sugar

½ cup butter

1 tablespoon flour

2 tablespoons milk

Preheat oven to 375° F. Have all ingredients at room temperature. Combine all the ingredients in a medium saucepan and cook over low heat until the butter is melted. Drop small teaspoons of the mixture 3 inches apart on a well-greased cookie sheet. Bake until golden brown, approximately 8-9 minutes. Cool slightly and remove from the cookie sheet with a small pancake lifter.

This recipe makes about 2 dozen thin, lacy cookies.

Gertie Tennant's cookie recipe is from
*Chow: From China to Canada: Memories of Food & Family*
by Janice Wong, Whitecap Books, 2005.

# Tamara's Chocolate Chip Cookies

Cream together:

**1 cup margarine**
**¾ cup white sugar**
**¾ cup brown sugar**

Mix in as well:

**1 egg**
**1 tsp. vanilla**

Mix in ½ cup at a time:

**2 ¼ cups white flour**
**½ tsp. baking soda**

Add:

**1 cup chocolate chips**

Using a teaspoon, roll a blob of batter in your hand and place on cookie sheet. Press down ball with two fingers. Bake at 350° F for 13 minutes. Take them out when they don't look done and they will be chewy and delicious.

Recipe from *The Gordon Cookbook,* Gordon School, Vancouver, 1999

# Satinder's Carrot Halwa

1 kilo carrots

2 litres milk

½ kilo sugar

200 grams ghee

50 grams crushed cashews

50 grams crushed almonds

10 grams grated cardamom

Wash and finely grate carrots. Boil grated carrots, sugar and milk in a pot, stirring until the milk evaporates and mixture thickens. Pour in ghee. Cook again for 10 minutes. Add grated cardamom and layer in a large tray. Garnish with crushed cashews and almonds. Leave at room temperature and cut into squares.

Recipe from **All India Sweets and Restaurant**, Vancouver